STEP 1 INTO READING®
STEP READY TO READ

D0441376

Wallykazam!™

Bath Party!

by Christy Webster
illustrated by David VanTuyle

Random House 🏠 New York

Gina Giant is having a party!

Dear Parents:

Congratulations! Your child is taking the first steps on an exciting journey. The destination? Independent reading!

STEP INTO READING® will help your child get there. The program offers five steps to reading success. Each step includes fun stories and colorful art or photographs. In addition to original fiction and books with favorite characters, there are Step into Reading Non-Fiction Readers, Phonics Readers and Boxed Sets, Sticker Readers, and Comic Readers—a complete literacy program with something to interest every child.

Learning to Read, Step by Step!

Ready to Read   Preschool–Kindergarten
• big type and easy words • rhyme and rhythm • picture clues
For children who know the alphabet and are eager to begin reading.

Reading with Help   Preschool–Grade 1
• basic vocabulary • short sentences • simple stories
For children who recognize familiar words and sound out new words with help.

Reading on Your Own   Grades 1–3
• engaging characters • easy-to-follow plots • popular topics
For children who are ready to read on their own.

Reading Paragraphs   Grades 2–3
• challenging vocabulary • short paragraphs • exciting stories
For newly independent readers who read simple sentences with confidence.

Ready for Chapters   Grades 2–4
• chapters • longer paragraphs • full-color art
For children who want to take the plunge into chapter books but still like colorful pictures.

STEP INTO READING® is designed to give every child a successful reading experience. The grade levels are only guides; children will progress through the steps at their own speed, developing confidence in their reading.

Remember, a lifetime love of reading starts with a single step!

Visit us on the Web!
StepIntoReading.com
randomhousekids.com

Educators and librarians, for a variety of teaching tools, visit us at RHTeachersLibrarians.com

ISBN 978-0-385-38767-5 (trade) — ISBN 978-0-385-38768-2 (lib. bdg.)

Printed in the United States of America   10 9 8 7 6 5 4 3 2

Dragons love parties.

Dragons also love mud!

Norville is muddy.

Muddy Norville wants to party!

He needs
to take a bath
before Gina's party.

Wally uses
his magic stick
to make a bathtub.

Dragons do not
like baths.

Wally holds up

his magic stick.

Wally makes the
bathtub bounce!

Bouncing baths
are fun!

Dragons still do not
like baths.

Norville hides.

Gina wants Norville
at her party.

Wally has an idea!

Wally uses
his magic stick.
He makes a band.

Wally makes balloons.

Wally makes bubbles!

It is a bath party!

Dragons love parties.

Dragons even
love parties
in the bath!